WORD BIRD'S EASTER WORDS

by Jane Belk Moncure

illustrated by Lois Axeman

Created by

THE CHILD'S WORLD

Library of Congress Cataloging in Publication Data

Moncure, Jane Belk.
 Word Bird's Easter words.

 (Word house words for early birds)
 Summary: Word Bird puts words about Easter in his
word house.
 1. Vocabulary—Juvenile literature. 2. Easter—
Juvenile literature. [1. Vocabulary. 2. Easter]
I. Axeman, Lois, ill. II. Title. III. Series:
Moncure, Jane Belk. Word house words for early birds.
PE1449.M5273 1987   428.1   87-13784
ISBN 0-89565-363-X

6 7 8 9 10 11 12 R 95 94

WORD BIRD'S EASTER WORDS

Word Bird made a...

word house.

"I will put Easter words
in my house," he said.

He put in these words—

new life

Easter lily

daffodils

violets

8

tulips

Easter flowers

duckling

bunnies

chicks

Easter pets

Easter bunny

Easter eggs

chocolate bunnies

chocolate eggs

Easter candy

jelly beans

marshmallow chicks

Easter-egg tree

Easter puppets

The Easter Bunny

His rabbity ears go flippity-flop
as he fills my basket to the top
with Easter treats for Easter day
Then he hippety-hops
away.

Easter verse

bunny hop

Easter baskets

Easter-egg hunt

Easter party

Easter bonnet

Easter suit

Easter parade

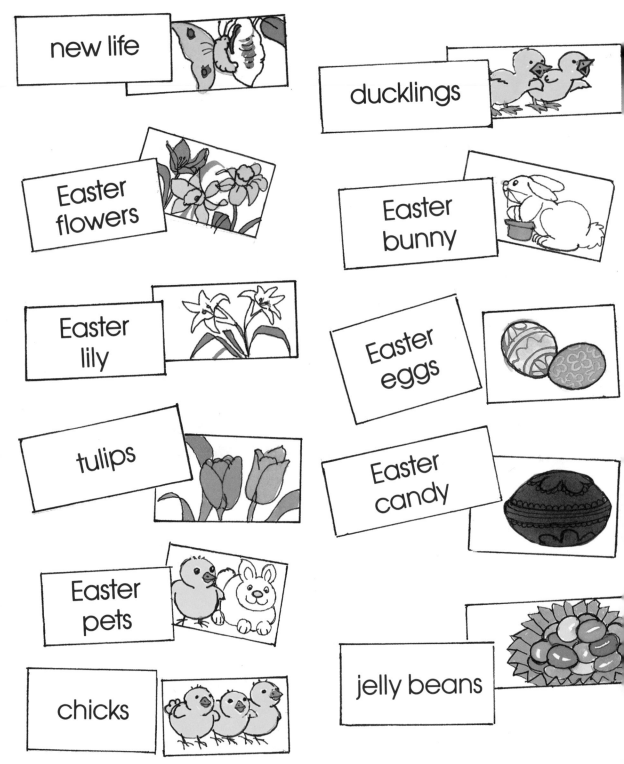

new life

ducklings

Easter flowers

Easter bunny

Easter lily

Easter eggs

tulips

Easter candy

Easter pets

chicks

jelly beans

...nese Easter words with **Word Bird** ?

Easter-egg tree

Easter-egg hunt

Easter puppets

Easter party

Easter verse

His rabbity ears go flippity flop

Easter bonnet

bunny hop

Easter suit

Easter baskets

Easter parade

You can make an Easter word house. You can put Word Bird's words in your house and read them too.

Can you think of other Easter words to put in your word house?